# Antony and Cleopatra

Sweet Cherry
Publishing

Published by Sweet Cherry Publishing Limited
Unit E, Vulcan Business Complex,
Vulcan Road,
Leicester, LE5 3EB,
United Kingdom

First published in the UK in 2012
2015 edition

ISBN: 978-1-78226-003-5

©Macaw Books

Title: Antony and Cleopatra

Lexile® code numerical measure L = Lexile® 1220L

Text & Illustrations by Macaw Books 2012

www.sweetcherrypublishing.com

Printed and bound by CPI Group (UK) Ltd, Croydon, CR0 4YY

# About Shakespeare

William Shakespeare, regarded as the greatest writer in the English language, was born in Stratford-upon-Avon in Warwickshire, England (around 23 April 1564). He was the third of eight children born to John and Mary Shakespeare.

Shakespeare was a poet, playwright and dramatist. He is often known as England's national poet and the 'Bard of Avon'. Thirty-eight plays, one hundred and fifty-four sonnets, two long narrative poems and several other poems are attributed to him. Shakespeare's plays have been translated into every major existent language and are performed more often than those of any other playwright.

**Mark Antony:** He is one of the three members of the triumvirate who rule the Roman Empire. He is a military general and in love with Cleopatra. He is torn between his duty to Rome and his love for Cleopatra.

**Cleopatra:** She is the Queen of Egypt and loves Mark Antony. She is powerful, attractive and dramatic. She uses her hold on Antony to manipulate him.

**Octavius Caesar:** He is the second member of the triumvirate. Octavius is the nephew and adopted son of Julius Caesar. He is ambitious, but lacks military skills.

**Sextus Pompeius (Pompey):** He is a threat to the triumvirate. He is young, popular and a skilled military general. He is unable to take advantage of political situations when they turn in his favour.

# Antony and Cleopatra

Rome was in a state of turmoil after the death of Julius Caesar. Brutus was on the run, along with Pompey, who had murdered Caesar. They were being hunted by the joint forces of Octavius Caesar, Julius Caesar's nephew, Mark Antony and Lepidus. Together, they managed to track down the evil perpetrators, and all the conspirators of Caesar's death were either killed, or they killed themselves rather than be captured by the new triumvirate.

Once Rome had been cleansed of the evil characters, the triumvirate decided to divide the Roman Empire, which now covered most of the globe, so that each of

the three lords had a portion of the empire to lord over. The gallant Mark Antony, the man responsible for bringing Caesar's killers to justice, was awarded the lands in Egypt, a place that was ruled by its own queen, Cleopatra.

Cleopatra was a shrewd woman, who knew that the only way to rule over her own people was to show her allegiance to the rulers in Rome.

Also, being perhaps the most beautiful woman in the whole of Egypt, she knew that it would be beneficial for her to show affection towards the various rulers, who were sent from Rome to take charge of affairs in Egypt.

The valiant queen had initially pretended to be in love with the great emperor, Julius Caesar himself. He had been in Egypt a few days before his death, and Cleopatra had warned him against going to Rome since she feared something terrible was about to happen to him. But Caesar had a knack for throwing caution to the wind, so he went anyway and was killed.

Cleopatra had learnt that Mark Antony was supposed to be the next Roman general who would take charge of the Egyptian state on behalf of the Roman Empire. She

immediately decided to woo
him and capture him with her
charms. This was not difficult for
Cleopatra because of her beauty.

Within a few days of his
arrival in Alexandria, Mark

Antony had fallen madly in love with Cleopatra. He was so enthralled by her charm that most people in the Roman camp felt that she must have carried out some sort of supernatural black magic on him. He neglected the affairs

of the state and spent all of his time in Cleopatra's chambers. Nothing could tear him away from her.

But then one day, news came from Rome of more unrest taking hold of the state. Sextus Pompey, the son of the great warlord Pompey, had long been looking for an opportunity to attack the state and take revenge for the death of his

father. He had always believed that his father and his friends were justified in conspiring to kill Julius Caesar, and therefore, he harboured the grief that the same state machinery had killed his father. Adding insult to injury, Octavius, Caesar's own

nephew, became the next
ruler of the Roman Empire.

Now was Sextus Pompey's
opportunity to strike. Mark
Antony, the backbone of the
Roman Army, was away in
Egypt, wrapped around the

enchantress Cleopatra's little
finger and Lepidus was in some
faraway land, ruling over his
share of the Roman Empire.
So only Octavius was left in
Rome, and everyone knew

he was not as great a warrior
as his uncle had been.

As soon as news of this
rebellion arrived, Octavius
Caesar, understanding the gravity
of the situation, immediately sent
a message to Antony ordering

him to return to Rome and help him prevent the riot that was about to commence. Cleopatra was not willing to let Antony leave, but the Roman general knew that he would have to go to the aid of Octavius, else word would get out that he stayed because of a woman. Obviously

this would not do, so he left
for Rome immediately.

Back in Rome, Mark
Antony learnt that his wife
had died quite some time ago.
Several messengers had been
sent to give him the news while
he was in Egypt, but he had
been so busy with Cleopatra
that he had refused to grant

them an audience, without even knowing the reason for their arrival. Antony now felt a sense of remorse for treating his wife with such disdain, when she had always loved him while she was alive. He was so shocked by the news that he forgot all about Cleopatra.

But now was not the time to regret past mistakes; there was a war to fight. Antony put on his armour at once and was soon by Octavius Caesar's side.

Octavius was very happy to see
Antony, because he knew that
without him, his army would be
unable to defeat Sextus Pompey.

In the end, a bloody war
did not have to be fought,
as Antony was able to bring
peace between Pompey and

Octavius. The two leaders agreed
to live amicably and called
off their respective armies
from engaging any further.

There was still the matter of
the growing animosity between
Antony and Octavius, though.

Octavius detested Antony, fearing that he was more popular with the people and a threat to his title. Antony, on the other hand, felt that Octavius had only got the title because of his relation to the great Julius Caesar, else it would surely have been bestowed on Antony himself. But a suitable gesture was negotiated to make peace between the two titular

leaders of the Roman Empire.
Since Antony's wife had died,
a matrimonial alliance was
organised between Antony and
Octavia, Octavius' sister.

There was another reason
for this alliance – now that he
had a powerful wife, everyone felt

that Antony would be immune to
the charms of Cleopatra and be
better able to focus on the daily
affairs of Egypt. Cleopatra, on
the other hand, upon receiving
news of Antony's marriage to

Octavia, was livid,
as she wanted to
have him all to
herself. She went
on a mad rampage,
breaking and

destroying everything around
her. Later, she calmed down and
reasoned that Antony did not
love Octavia, the marriage merely
a political ploy to ease matters
between Octavius and Antony.

Antony, now having
forgotten Cleopatra, left to

administer Athens for a while
and Octavia accompanied him.
But matters did not continue
that way for long. Without
the expert services of
Antony, Pompey and
Caesar were soon at
each other's throats

and it seemed that a
war would have to be
fought after
all. News reached
Antony in Athens
that both parties were
preparing their armies
for war, which obviously
meant that Antony
would have to head
back to Rome and join
the forces of Octavius
Caesar. He immediately
sent his wife Octavia
back to Rome to be of
service to her troubled
brother, and then the
great general himself fled
to Egypt to be reunited

with the ruler of his heart, Cleopatra.

When news of Antony's departure for Egypt reached Octavius Caesar, he was naturally

furious. He could not believe
that his uncle's closest aide had
left him to his own devices
under the threat of war and
gone away to woo a subject
queen! He put off the war with
Sextus Pompey and immediately

declared war on Antony and Cleopatra. Within a few days, Antony found the mighty Roman Army before him in Egypt.

Being a soldier, Octavius Caesar offered Antony the chance to decide how he wanted to fight the war. Antony, perhaps making the biggest mistake of his entire life, decided to fight the Romans at sea, not knowing the Egyptian Navy would be no match for the might of

the Roman Navy. Moreover,
the Roman Navy was present
in full force because they had
sailed all the way from Rome
to Egypt. Had Antony chosen
to fight them over land, the
Egyptian Army would perhaps

have had a greater chance of
defeating Octavius Caesar.

As was expected, the
Egyptians could not
bear the brunt of the
Roman Navy, and
within a short while
they were falling

apart. Antony tried his best to revive the men and fight his way through the ranks, but with their morale broken, there was little that even the great Antony could do. Unable to direct his men against the Roman fleet, he too was forced to fall back and retreat with them. Caesar had won the war, but he still chased Antony into the palace in Alexandria.

As Antony reached the palace, he found a note from Cleopatra. It said that she had felt let down by his inability to win the war and had therefore consumed poison and killed herself. But Cleopatra was not

dead at all. She had merely gone
to hide in a tomb not far from
the palace. Perhaps she felt that
if Antony thought she was dead,
he would no longer try to fight

with Octavius Caesar and the
war would be stopped. This
was perhaps the only way out
of her current predicament.

But Antony was truly in love with her, and when he read the letter he was heartbroken. With Cleopatra dead he had nothing left to live for. Taking out his dagger, Antony tried to stab himself to death, but only managed to wound himself.

When his followers
found him, they
immediately carried him
off to the tomb where
Cleopatra was hiding.

When he was finally
in Cleopatra's arms, Antony

succumbed to his injuries
and breathed his last breath.

Cleopatra could
not help but
hold herself
responsible for
his death, since

she knew that he had tried to
take his own life after reading her
letter. She was so overcome with
grief that she decided to end her
own life. She also realised that
with Antony dead, there would
be no one to save her in the

event that Octavius Caesar found her. Therefore, Cleopatra sent for some of the most poisonous snakes in the whole of Egypt, and let them bite her. Very soon she too lay dead, next to her beloved Antony. Octavius Caesar found the two of them dead inside the tomb, but he did not turn out to be as cold-hearted as Cleopatra had thought he was.

Praising the valiant Antony's bravery and also the beauty of Cleopatra, Octavius Caesar asked his men to bury the lovers together. This was the immortal love story of the noble Mark Antony and his beautiful Cleopatra.